Cinema
Mon Amour

Dr. Omkar Bhatkar

Ukiyoto Publishing

All global publishing rights are held by

Ukiyoto Publishing

Published in 2023

Content Copyright © Dr. Omkar Bhatkar
Cover Photograph by Berges Santok
ISBN 9789360490270

All rights reserved.
No part of this publication may be reproduced,
transmitted, or stored in a retrieval system, in any
form by any means, electronic, mechanical,
photocopying, recording or otherwise, without the
prior permission of the publisher.

The moral rights of the author have been asserted.

This is a work of fiction. Names, characters, businesses, places, events, locales, and incidents are either the products of the author's imagination or used in a fictitious manner. Any resemblance to actual persons, living or dead, or actual events is purely coincidental.

This book is sold subject to the condition that it shall not by way of trade or otherwise, be lent, resold, hired out or otherwise circulated, without the publisher's prior consent, in any form of binding or cover other than that in which it is published.

www.ukiyoto.com

For the love of
Yasujiro Ozu
Terrence Malick
Andrei Tarkovsky

Dedicated to
Amita Valmiki
P.S Vivek
Kanchana Mahadevan

Wyomia Almeida

Writer-Director's Note

Time is what you make of it. Memories remain. What does one do with time when it's gone? How does time affect each one of us? Similarly, how do films affect us? Do the films that we watch shape our psyche? These are the sort of questions that Cinema Mon Amour deals with. Cinema Mon Amour is a self-explanatory title, expressing love for films, especially those of Abbas Kiarostami, Andrei Tarkovsky, Terrence Malick and Yasujiro Ozu. Cinema Mon Amour is a play for cinephiles and there are many reference points to film-makers in the play. More than a story it's a situational play about an estranged couple meeting after 14 years to talk about life, the passage of time and films that they love. The meeting is an attempt to find something gone astray. Do they find it? (The relationship from the beginning between the couple is ambiguous and therefore the reader/director needs to take care while perceiving that it remains that way). The play is written keeping in mind Film as Philosophy juxtaposing the thought with cinema as a reflection of life and life as an intimation of cinema. Cinema Mon Amour tries to grapple with life, cinema, philosophy and poetry in the same breath. The entire play is in one scene.

The play at several points refers to characters from films that both of them remember. However, it would be the task of the reader/director to interpret them. For instance, the Girl from Nevers is a reference to the character from the film Hiroshima Mon Amour by Alain Resnais. *50-50, very very tasty-tasty is a popular jingle of Television commercial in 90's India. Films of Ingmar Bergman, Andrei Tarkovsky, Yasujiro Ozu, Abbas Kiarostami, Terrence Malick.

The play, if staged, can be accompanied by lilting acoustic guitar (Live or pre-recorded) for emotional sequences and blackouts. The songs mentioned in the play are suggestive, the Director is free to choose music of their choice.

For public performances and staging of the play kindly get in touch on

metamorphosistheatreinc@gmail.com

Characters

He

He is about 36-38 years old and is working as a consultant for a book publishing firm dealing in educational literature for children. He studied commerce for his undergraduate studies, followed by Philosophy for his Master and then completed his MBA in Public Relations. He lives a busy life on weekdays and there are weekends when he doesn't work and tries to make time for things he loves like watching plays, and films and attending music concerts. He plays guitar when he is in the mood and has now even picked up the ukulele. There is an emptiness in his life but he has enough ways to fill that emptiness. He comes across as a very gentle and polite person, it's only rarely when he gets triggered that he forgets his gentleness. He thinks when necessary and when he doesn't have solutions about something, he tries his best not to worry and leave it for time to handle, that's a different thing worry doesn't leave him and therefore he tends to lose his smile in that bargain.

She

She is about 36-38 years old and is working as an Adjunct faculty in Philosophy at an undergraduate college/university. Her interest in teaching includes Film as Philosophy, Epistemology, Phenomenology and Aesthetics. She has studied

Philosophy for her undergraduate as well as post-graduate studies and intends to work on a Ph.D. She lives a life that as much is organised is also chaos because she is committed to several projects all at the same time. She is probably writing an academic paper for a journal, reviewing a book, attending a conference, planning her class, selecting the reference books for the syllabus, attending to domestic duties and family, and attending a film festival, all at the same time. She talks affirmatively but also politely sharp. She is a quick decision-maker and knows what she is looking for. She doesn't spend too much time thinking over things and she is equally in love with romance.

Contents

Scene I — 1

About the Author — 40

Scene I

The College Courtyard

(In the college courtyard, he had been waiting for quite some time. He spends time looking at the college building and remembering the bygone days. He keeps waiting and then when there is nothing to do, he reminisces about playing guitar in his college days. He opens his guitar and plays until she arrives and watches him play)

He :

As usual, you're late

She :

As usual, you're on time.

(They both smile)

She :

So how come you thought of this one

He :

What do you mean by this one

She :

I mean how did you think of meeting all of a sudden?

He :

aaaaaaa..... Just like that

She :

Why should they be the reason?

He   :

Yeah, that's also true why should there be a reason?

She   :

But I am glad that you thought about this, college days feel a little different.

He :

And there is something that is still similar

She   :

Yes, it's different and still similar

He   :

Maybe we are different and yet alike.

She   :

You mean both of us?

He   :

No, not both of us. Leave it.

She:

No, say.

He   :

No, let's leave it.

She:

No, say

(They both laugh)

He :

So, we have already started behaving like how we used to be.

She :

Were you expecting something different

He :

I wasn't expecting anything

She :

You thought I wouldn't come

He :

No, I was certain you would

She :

Every certainty is also uncertainty

He :

You already started

She :

Should I be waiting for Christmas then?

He :

You still sound similar?

She :

Are you expecting something different?

He :

I wasn't expecting anything

She :

Looks like you have come with no expectations at all.

He :

Do you have any?

She :

What?

He :

Do you have any expectations?

She :

About what

He :

I see you have already started.

She :

I did tell you I'm not waiting for Christmas.

He :

But you would in college days?

She :

That was then

He :

It's different now?

She :

*50 - 50

He   :

*Very very tasty tasty.

(they laugh)

She   :

You still make those silly jokes

He   :

If you talk rhetorically like you used to, why can't I make silly jokes?

She   :

so, I see, not much has changed.

He   :

Only time can tell that.

She   :

"True, time is a state: The flame in which there lives the salamander of the human soul".

He   :

Tarkovsky,

She   :

Smarty pants.

(He gets up, looks at himself, at his pants and says)

He   :

Really!

She :

How can a person talk about Tarkovsky and crack silly jokes in the same breath?

He :

Just like the way there is suffering in the world,

He :

Oh wait, let me rephrase, just like how there is profound suffering in the world and yet people believe in the omnipotence of God.

She :

Precisely

He :

What do you mean precisely?

She :

Precisely, because there is a profound suffering there is much more belief in the omnipotence of God, if there was no suffering, do you think people would have believed in God, let me put it this way if there was no profound suffering do you think people would have believed in the omnipotent of God?

He :

Reminds me of Amit's lectures

She :

Reminds, *(pauses, recollects)* Remembering is a memory and time and memory are like two sides of the same coin. Without time there is no memory and without memory, there is no time.

He :

So, I see, you are still obsessed with the idea of memory and even time.

She :

Why do you think I still carry Tarkovsky with me, wherever I go?

He :

I am a little perplexed, rather surprised that at least Tarkovsky remained timeless for you

She :

Should I take it as a compliment? Or are you hinting at something else?

He :

I just commented and I don't think I have any undertones behind them.

He :

Why do you always have to look for something else in everything?

She :

Because there is always a shadow lurking under the lamp.

He :

I thought I was the one who was the Pessimistic amongst us.

She :

So, you admit that you were? Are you still the same way?

He :

How would I know, before you go you tell me if I am the same way?

She :

I think we are putting too much pressure on time, poor time!

He :

Time is certainly not poor, memory is.

She :

And why would you say that?

He :

Time you can at least try ways to define it and you can locate it in the realm of existence, rather our existence depends on time but memory is different, it's like a mystical experience you can't explain it for yourself, and we don't understand it.

She :

14 years seems to have affected you.

He :

Rather its time, time has had its effect on us.

She :

I cannot deny that, there are parts of me that I understand and parts that I don't and each part is an effect of time.

He :

So, you do see that time and memory are interlinked, as if time is the cause and memory, is the effect. The cause cannot be discarded at any cost and therefore time remains hanging all around us like a shadow of the memory.

She :

We are still talking similarly like we used to 14 years ago, even in these columns this ground is still the same even though we in a way have touched everything around us and it has changed something about us.

She :

Are you in touch with Amit?

He :

No, I have lost touch with everyone.

She :

You don't even use Facebook; how do you expect you would remain in touch with people?

He :

Didn't People remain in touch before Facebook existed

She :

They did, but Facebook just makes it easier to connect to people

He :

If that was the case, I don't think we all would have been lonely.

She :

No, that's another story altogether.

She :

Aren't you with someone now?

He :

At the moment I am with you. *(Slight smile)*

She :

And after this moment. *(Slight smile)*

He :

With myself. *(Slight smile)*

She :

And after that? *(Slight smile)*

He :

Still with myself. *(smile)*

She :

Will there be another movement when you are not with yourself? *(smile)*

He :

That would probably be death. *(laughingly)*

She :

Now, that's farfetched. *(he smiles)*

He :

Do you want to know If I'm single or not? Then ask... *(Sweetly smiling)*

She :

Are you single? *(Smilingly)*

He :

Will it make a difference?

She :

This is the reason I was not asking you.

He :

I am *(He adds quickly)*

He :

But when I was married, you didn't want me then? So, what's the point of being single? *(smiles)*

He :

How about you?

She :

How about we don't talk about this at all?

He :

That's convenient.

He :

You ask me the same question and you expect an answer but when I ask you, you simply say let's not talk about it?

She :

....

(She goes to say something.... he interrupts)

He :

But now please don't answer because I don't think I deserve this answer. It's not coming from you. The moment you would answer now it would sound like a deal which of course I don't want it to sound like...

He :

(After a long pause)

I am sorry, we already started our usual banter, I thought after so many years some things would have changed.

(Silence)

(Both remain quiet for a few moments and he eventually strums his guitar. He plays on his guitar

(♪) Ben Howard – Promise (Visuals) (♪) and as the song is about the fade, she begins talking)

She :

This makes me feel alive. I feel free, I like this

She :

How have you been all these years?

He :

It's so strange, usually people ask this question the moment they meet but I guess there is always something unusual about us.

He :

How are you, have you been?

(Long silence)

He :

I like this silence; this shortage of words that can't express how we feel about or how we have been!

She :

You know that words can't express everything we feel, words are flaccid.

He :

Are you working somewhere?

She :

It's been a complicated journey, I thought I would pursue teaching and I did start with teaching just that I couldn't survive there.

He :

You're making teaching sound like a corporate job

She :

I don't know which is better. But experiencing one side of it, I can surely say that it's a very egoistic place. It was my illusion that studying Liberal Arts and especially philosophy can make people more down to earth, more loving, more caring and recognizing the other as one of us. I used to think that there would be fewer walls, divisions, frontiers and labels but I was wrong, I was just wrong.

He :

Were the walls so strong that you didn't want to stay in them?

She :

I can always pursue philosophy but not only through academics and teaching.

He :

What do you mean by that?

She :

I can make films

He :

Never thought so,

She :

What, That I could make films

He :

No, that you would like to make films

She :

(a little apologetically) I didn't know it myself, but I would like to explore. Maybe then I will discover if this is what I am supposed to do.

He :

Has this inspiration come from Terence Malick?

She :

Watching his films strengthened my thoughts.

He :

I would be delighted to see your work. I would like to be in the First row watching your creation.

She :

I feel good when you say that, it matters so much.

(silence)

She :

where were you this long?

He :

This evening will turn into eternity if we start telling our stories, yours and mine, maybe we will keep them for some other day for now just let us be in this moment.

She :

Sometimes I feel you are a stranger.

He :

That is why we could open ourselves to each other.

He :

What kind of films would you be making?

He :

Will it be simple like Ozu or complicated like Malick?

She :

Maybe a blend of both.

He :

You remember that day when Amit mam screened 'Taste of Cherry' in the class, and we were all discussing the death of Mr Badi as she would say when we all were having our versions of the climax and she came up with this understanding of the Sufi term *tasawuff,* and everything just fell in place. The class was quiet, and there was a sense of completeness, it made sense, and the void of the incompleteness was filled with a sense of something indescribable.

She :

And you remember when Kanchana mam was talking about the passion of Joan of Arc, that was one screening I shall never forget. It has left a deep impact on me, possibly one of the earlier films that planted the seeds of my passion for cinema rather than for life!

He :

I miss those days,

She :

(Adding immediately) Terribly. *(Reminiscing)* There was something magical in the air as if we were floating two inches above the ground and when college was over those two inches disappeared and our feet started touching the ground.

He :

Then, we felt liberated and free and now there is a sense of burden.

She :

But don't you feel your burden is lighter than those around you who did not pursue liberal Arts?

He :

Aren't you being discriminatory?

She :

No, I am just trying to talk about the beauty of pursuing literature, cinema, poetry, and philosophy. It has certainly contributed to making us better beings, not in a discriminatory sense but more humane, more questioning, more critical

She :

I only wish that if they made us spend more time with art, artists, and their works then probably ego would have been replaced by the ability to appreciate, to love and to connect with each other.

He :

Are you disillusioned with academics?

She :

I had some expectations, but no complaints anymore

He :

What is that you desire?

She :

Nothing much now.

He :

Really,

She :

Yeah, no desires.

He :

Yeah or No

She :

No

She :

What do you desire?

He :

Only if we could find what we love.

She :

Aaaa, I think you need to slightly tweak what you're saying.

He :

How?

She :

Maybe, only if you could find what you desire?

He :

Isn't love desire?

She :

No

He :

How so? Love is a feeling, and so is desire, a feeling for something.

She :

For something to be fulfilled?

He :

Yes.

She :

Desire is directed to an object that is desired.

She :

Love is directed to an object or even a subject that could be loved.

She :

Desire ends when the goal is met, desires are fulfilled, and one feels a sense of satisfaction of the desire which is not the case with love. Love isn't passive, unlike desire. Love is becoming, the subject-object merging, in an activity, a processual process.

He :

Sorry, what

She :

Love means never having to say you're sorry. *(She smiles)*

He :

Here you go again, this becoming of love reminds me of a short, frail professor we had. I remember some of his classes on Theistic Mysticism.

She :

You never liked that class.

He :

Actually, I just could not get his classes.

She :

And you just couldn't get Kierkegaard's realm.

He :

Something was with that man; you remember that hilarious quote He used to often say:

She :

I know which one you're saying. Give me a moment, I'll tell you

She :

"Marry, and you will regret it; don't marry, you will also regret it; marry or don't marry, you will regret it either way. Laugh at the world's foolishness, you will regret it; weep over it, you will regret that too; laugh at the world's foolishness or weep over it, you will regret both. Believe a woman,

He :

you will regret it;

She :

believe her not,

He :

you will also regret it…

She :

Hang yourself, you will regret it; do not hang yourself,

He   :

and you will regret that too;

She   :

hang yourself or don't hang yourself, you'll regret it either way;

Together   :

whether you hang yourself or do not hang yourself, you will regret both. This, gentlemen, is the essence of all philosophy."

(In the neighbouring compound there is a sound check going on for some party or wedding reception and suddenly (♪) Silhouettes of You by Isaac Gracie (♪) starts playing loudly. They both look at each other with a sad smile. While the song is playing, they keep quiet and decide to surrender to that moment without speaking and gazing at each other intermittently. She takes out a broken mirror from her bag and looks at herself)

He   :

Your mirror is broken

She   :

I know

He   :

Someone special gifted it, it looks like that

She :

Kind of ...

(pauses, looks at him)

She :

I gifted it to myself

He :

Then why don't you buy a new one?

She :

I like it this way, it reminds me of my selves.

She :

Where do you live now?

She :

I still live near Five Gardens

He :

How about you I am at Worli

She :

So, you haven't shifted

He :

There was no reason

He :

Even you haven't

She :

There was no reason

He :

Do you still live with your family?

She :

I do, with my parents.

She :

And You,

He :

No, I'm alone now

She :

Are you happy at home alone?

He :

I don't think I would have been happier if I was with someone.

She :

Don't you feel the need for someone to be there?

He :

I do, but not every moment. There are moments when I like to be alone.

She :

How about those when you want someone next to you?

(Light gradually changes to blue to the trickle of raindrops, He gets up and moves as per his comfort)

He   :

Those are the terrible moments, a kind of blueness that shed its dark cloud on my home and it's raining inside the house, drenching everything in its blueness.

(She gets up and moves as per her comfort)

She   :

And is it only your home where it rains like this?

He   :

It seems so…

She   :

No, not really, sometimes the clouds move from your house and park themselves above mine.

He   :

Then what do you do?

She   :

I get wet under it.

He   :

Why don't you carry an umbrella? *(Asking innocently)*

She   :

Umbrellas are designed for outdoors, when it rains inside and only you can see this rain, who will design umbrellas for your indoor rain?

Do you have an umbrella?

He :

No, even I get drenched,

She :

And then

He :

And then I run my fingers over the drenched memories and everything sprouts in pale blue leaves under the cobalt blue sky.

She :

To that, I play, *(she quickly scrolls through her phone and plays the song)* (♪) Ghostly Kisses – The City Hold My Heart (♪)

(She lets the song play for a few moments and then he continues….)

He :

You never know when this rain will stop raining above your home. After all the attempts I try to go to sleep soaked in sweat and rain. I try hard to sleep but sleep refuses to meet me when it rains profusely, as if even sleep can't sleep under this blue rain.

She :

I know, I need to find a way, find a way out of this, But I doubt, and can't just put my faith in one place. I wonder how I would sail tonight, how I would go on living. I just don't stay true to my beliefs.

He :

At least, you have something to believe at some point. I need to fill this big, black hole in me.

He :

My beliefs just keep changing.

She :

That's what I'm trying to say, I can't stay firm on my beliefs, they keep oscillating like a pendulum. And I oscillate hanging on it, neither her, nor there.

He :

Like the girl from Nevers, stuck between Hiroshima and France, not knowing what is real and what is memory.

He :

Fortunately, If I fall asleep, I try to just keep sleeping. As if sleep is real and this world is a dream from which I live here for brief moments to go back to my sleeping wish.

She :

My soul is wounded; I can't take any more sadness, no more disappointments, no more rejections. I never thought life would be a daily suffering …..

He :

You make yourself sound like a goddess of sorrows as if it's only your heart that is bleeding. Your tears can be seen, is it why you're deeply sad? What about the pain of a heart like mine which couldn't even cry at times when I should have cried and now, I cry when I lose an email!

She :

I never said your pain is lesser than mine,

He :

You carry a broken mirror to remind yourself of the broken you, what should I carry?

She :

Carry something so I can take notice.

He :

To notice things, you need to pay attention.

She :

You always go on the same track; I thought some things would have at least changed. Some things you would have learnt

He :

Why should the learning be reserved for others and teaching be left to you? You are the teacher and the other, the learner. You are the subject and the world your object, why should everything move around it? Why don't you not take the central position for some time?

She :

Time, we are back to time?

He :

It's true, there is no escape from time. Wish you could have decentred yourself for at least some moments.

She :

I've done that enough, I've lost enough of myself now there is a paltry scrap, and I need it. I'm alone and I need that to stay alive.

He :

You know, the world is full of lonely people.

She :

I know, *(pause)* Life is disappointing

He :

But can you answer in the affirmative like Noriko?

She :

Wish one day, I could.

He :

I too dreamed of becoming important to someone, someday.

She :

You were important to me.

He :

I know, Were.......

She :

I thought somebody like you could make things alright for me.

He :

I too thought the same someday, someone could make things alright for me.

She :

Probably, we were waiting in vain.

Together :

Probably

She :

Waiting is also time-centric; we don't know who waited for how long.

He :

And who got impatient?

She :

And who started looking elsewhere for love?

He :

I wanted a breather.

She :

I wanted love

He :

I wanted life

She :

That's what you went looking around for ......

He :

Didn't you even look for it?

She :

Why are we talking about this?

He :

Wasn't a philosopher's heart enough that you need a poet's bed

She :

Only if you knew a poet is a philosopher

He :

But is a philosopher a poet?

……..

He :

Is a poet's bed different? Is it filled with fake flowers and words that are meaningless?

She :

How convenient is it to use Derrida when you want and discard it when you like?

He :

Words rendered meaningless are not solely proprietary of Derrida or Barthes.

He :

Tell me is a poet's bed different, is it king's size? Or maybe the poet's way of love is so ethereal that my love felt so little in front of it.

She :

Only if you knew that Love is not something that happens between the legs and is limited to a king's king-size bed.

He :

Don't tell me now that Love can be beyond sex.

She :

Why do we still talk about love and sex in the same breath?

He :

Don't tell me, now you're looking for platonic love. If that was the case then my philandering shouldn't have been the cause of any of the consequences

She :

I was different then,

He :

What do you mean you were different?

She :

You won't understand?

He :

The classic you, where nobody understands you, the Hegelian goddesses, often misinterpreted and misread.

(Silence)

He :

You know I loved you.

She :

I loved you too,

He :

Were you taking a sort of revenge?

She :

Don't belittle my love, I would never do something of that kind.

He :

Then how of all the people, you chose him to be with…..You really loved him? Or was it sex?

She :

Didn't he tell you anything?

He :

I won't reveal that, that's between him and me.

She :

Are you in touch with him?

He :

I said I won't answer anything about him.

She :

I'm sure you would be and you should be, you knew each other for years after all.

He :

I won't talk about him.

She :

To relieve you from the torments of the past I must admit love and sex are two different things, they don't necessarily come together. And Love unifies but Sex separates.

He :

Now, where did you get that from?

(She smiles with a raised eyebrow)

He :

It surely must be one of the postmodernists. *(smirks)*

She :

Can we not talk about this; I have moved far away from all this.

He :

Like the girl from Nevers, who could never leave Nevers?

He :

I feel I'm fortunate to be a pessimist. I always imagine the worst that can happen. So that there is nothing to fear.

She :

I have known you from the time you have lived in that black hole.

He :

But you have no clue, what's happened to the black hole in fourteen years?

She :

I tried to at least stay in touch.

He :

Touch, I see.

She :

Don't mock that. But some people feel like they want to be detached, they can't put their armour down, they want to carry the weight of it wherever they go and then quietly they walk away into empty spaces, sealing the fissures.

He :

I have made that mistake once with you of putting my armour down, I couldn't do it again. I can't take that chance…

She :

You sound like the Meetic dating site, ads I saw in Paris which go advertising; Get Love without Chance', 'Be in love without falling in love', how is it even possible? Love is a chance rather than a continuous chance because Love is a continuous process rather than a one-time event that happens.

He :

The Hegelian goddess, philosophizing love. *(says in a neutral manner)*

She :

You do know that I find it demeaning when you do that.

(She takes a few steps to move away and he says)

He :

I'm sorry, *(She stops and keeps standing, without looking at him)* I'm not demeaning you, that's what you never realized. I say these words but there is no sarcasm behind it. It is you who interprets it as sarcastic. I simply say it without belittling you, have you ever realized how complicated it is to be with you, because you're this.

(She turns around and responds)

She :

What is this?

He :

You're so clear and

She :

And

He :

And so ambiguous…..

(silence)

She :

You're not different either, there is discipline and anarchy in the way you function, I too don't understand you.

She :

Wish we could not be burdened with the desire to understand, possibly then we could just love

He :

You could still love by dropping the need to understand.

She :

I've passed that time for it, now I can't return there and even if I do, I won't be the same I.

He :

I just want you to know one thing before we go. Getting to be around you was the best thing that ever happened to me

She :

I came here to spend time with you, to find the 'I' that 'I'm' no more. When you called up yesterday asking to meet in the college courtyard, I for a brief moment saw a part of me in the mirror that I had not seen for the last fourteen years. Like Rimbaud I came here to re-invent love, not realizing I would also be meeting the same you and the same me that I don't want to meet. What a loss to spend that much time with someone, only to find out that he's the same person you knew and you hope time would have changed a few things.

He :

Time did change a few things but not entirely.

(They both start moving away from each other very slowly and the song plays in the background. Here, (♪) Bloom by Paper Kites (Credits) (♪) can be used)

(Light fades to blackout. He is still on the stage and she has walked away in the audience)

He :

After all she did, I still love her. *(To himself)*

(She says from the audience with her back facing him and the stage)

She :

I came because he is all that I have. *(To herself)*

(CURTAIN)

"What if everything in the world were a misunderstanding, what if laughter were really tears?"

— **Soren Kierkegaard**

About the Author

Dr. Omkar Bhatkar is a Sociologist with a doctoral thesis concerned with Proxemics and Social Ecology. He has been a visiting professor for a decade now teaching Film Theory, Culture Studies, and Gender Studies. He has also served as a faculty for the London School of Economics International Programmes in Sociology.

He is the Co-Founder and Head of the eclectic 'St. Andrew's Centre for Philosophy and Performing Arts which constantly strives to bridge art and academics. Dr. Omkar Bhatkar runs his theatre group known as Metamorphosis Theatre Inc. His works largely focus on Poetry in Motion, Existentialist Themes, and Contemporary French Plays in Translation. He has written and directed more than twenty plays, several of which have been performed at Art and Theatre Festivals. In collaboration with Alliance Française de Bombay, he has directed several Contemporary French Plays in English. He is also a Stage Critic and reviews plays. Dr Bhatkar's play 'Blue Storm' was selected at the Asia Playwrights Theatre Festival 2021 held in South Korea. 'Blue Storm' was also an invitation play at the International Women's Theatre Festival 2021 held in Incheon, South Korea.

Though he is grounded in theatre, he also explores the world of films. As a filmmaker, he has written and directed independent feature films like Perhaps Tea, The Farewell Band, Testament of Emily, and also a poetic documentary titled 'Painted Hymns: The Chapels of Santa Monica'. Recently, he made an experimental feature film titled 'Time, Distance, Memory on the Feather of a Wing'

He is a thalassophile who finds solace by drowning in the depths of poetry and spends his waking life painting, reading, writing, and engaging in conversations over black tea.

www.ingramcontent.com/pod-product-compliance
Lightning Source LLC
LaVergne TN
LVHW041638070526
838199LV00052B/3437